MONSTER SLEEPOVER!

Scott Beck

Abrams Books for Young Readers
New York

Artist's note:
The art in this book was created with acrylic paint on illustration board.

Library of Congress Cataloging-in-Publication Data

Beck, Scott.
Monster sleepover! / by Scott Beck.
p. cm.
Summary: Doris throws a slumber party for Ben and her other monster friends, complete with games, snacks, and an effort to stay up all night.
ISBN 978-0-8109-4059-8
[1. Sleepovers—Fiction. 2. Parties—Fiction. 3. Monsters—Fiction.] I. Title.
PZ7.B3809Mon 2009
[E]—dc22
2009000317

Text and illustrations copyright © 2009 Scott Beck

Book design by Chad W. Beckerman and Melissa Arnst

Published in 2009 by Abrams Books for Young Readers,
an imprint of Harry N. Abrams, Inc.

Printed and bound in China
10 9 8 7 6 5 4 3 2 1

Abrams Books for Young Readers are available at special discounts when purchased in quantity for premiums and promotions as well as fundraising or educational use. Special editions can also be created to specification. For details, contact specialmarkets@hnabooks.com or the address below.

HNA ■■■■■
harry n. abrams, inc.
a subsidiary of La Martinière Groupe
115 West 18th Street
New York, NY 10011
www.hnabooks.com

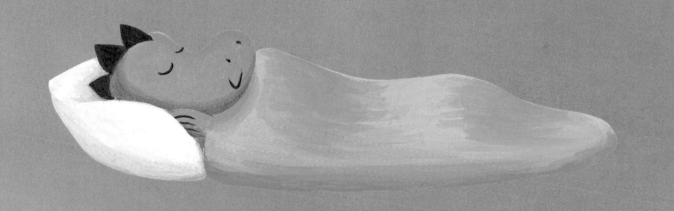

Doris is cleaning up.

Is she getting ready for a party?

Let's see . . . pajamas . . . sleeping bags . . .

Oh, it IS a party! It's a sleepover party!

Let's play Simon Says.
Simon says wave!

Simon says jump up . . .

and stay there!

We have a winner!

Doris can tell the future.

Someone looks hungry.

Oh look, Robot wants to sing a song.

Very good, Robot!

Is the sprinkler on?

WHAT are you doing? Go play in the house!

That's not what I meant!

Hey! Hey! Hey!

Settle down!

AND NO MORE FIGHTING!

Now you two kiss
and make up.

That's it! Bedtime!

Everybody go to sleep!

GO to sleep!

GO TO SLEEP!

Good night, sleep tight, and don't bite the bedbugs tonight!

And tomorrow you'll have a very big appetite!

Ben thinks that was quite a party. When he gets home . . .

he sends Doris a very nice thank-you note to tell her so.